TENTH ANNIVERSARY WISHES

TENTH ANNIVERSARY WISHES

edited by Catherine Kouts and Laura Cavaluzzo
photography by Elisabeth Fall

GIBBS·SMITH
P
PUBLISHER
Salt Lake City

First Edition
99 98 97 96   5 4 3 2 1

This is a Peregrine Smith Book, published by
Gibbs Smith, Publisher
P.O. Box 667
Layton, UT 84041

Design by The Stiebling Group
In-house editing by Dawn Valentine Hadlock
Cover photograph by Elisabeth Fall

Library of Congress Cataloging-in-Publication Data

Tenth anniversary wishes / edited by Catherine Kouts and Laura Cavaluzzo ;
    photography by Elisabeth Fall. — 1st ed.
        p.   cm.
    "This is a Peregrine Smith book"—T.p. verso.
    ISBN 0-87905-651-7
    1. Marriage—Quotations, maxims, etc.   I. Kouts, Catherine.
II. Cavaluzzo, Laura.
PN6084.M3T46   1996
306.81—dc20   96-16569
                                                         CIP

Printed and bound in Singapore

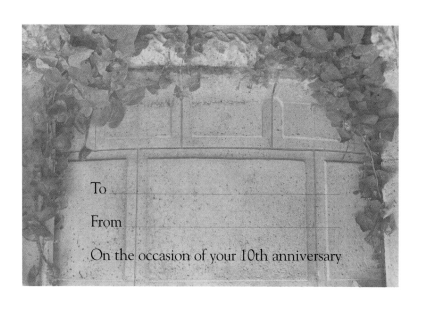

To _____

From _____

On the occasion of your 10th anniversary

In the beginning . . .

The Book of Life begins with
a man and a woman in a garden.
It ends with Revelation.

Oscar Wilde, A Woman of No Importance

Love consists in this, that two solitudes protect
and touch and greet each other.

Rainer Maria Rilke, Letters to a Young Poet

I shall not blush to tell you that you have made the whole world
besides so indifferent to me that, if I cannot be yours, they may
dispose of me as they please.

Dorothy Osborne, in a letter to Sir William Temple

IT IS SO PLEASANT TO BEGIN IN COMPLETE
IGNORANCE AND THEN TO LEARN SO MANY REASONS
FOR GIVING NERVOUS LAUGHS AND NERVOUS CRIES,
FOR UTTERING LITTLE MUFFLED MOANS, WITH YOUR
TOES CURLED UP WITH TENSION.

Colette, Claudine Married

TREMENDOUS FORCES . . .
STONE-PILED FENCE
ALL TUMBLED DOWN
BY TWO CATS IN LOVE

Shiki, Cherry Blossoms: Japanese Haiku Series III

THIS IS LOVE: TO FLY TOWARD A SECRET SKY,
TO CAUSE A HUNDRED VEILS TO FALL EACH MOMENT.

Jelaluddin Rumi, Ruins of the Heart

FOR IN MY MIND, OF ALL MANKIND
I LOVE BUT YOU ALONE.

Anonymous, "The Nut Brown Maid"

I was at a party feeling very shy because there were a lot of celebrities around, and I was sitting in a corner alone and a very beautiful young man came up to me and offered me some salted peanuts and he said, "I wish they were emeralds" as he handed me the peanuts and that was the end of my heart. I never got it back.

Helen Hayes, in an interview with a Hollywood reporter

My Charlie's life was composed almost entirely of brilliant curtain lines. . . . It wasn't enough that he poured the peanuts . . . into my trembling hands. He had to add, "I wish they were emeralds."

Of course, I was bowled over. Starting with Mother, that evening, I told everyone who would listen all about it. When in Hollywood, some years later, I wanted to be cooperative with an interviewer and I repeated it again, the line was committed to print. From that moment on, it was to haunt us. Even as late as our tenth anniversary . . . we found a bowl of dyed-green peanuts awaiting us on our table. Such antics over the years so depressed Charlie that, at the end of World War II, returning from India and the Eastern Theater, he dumped a bag of emeralds in my lap.

"I wish they were peanuts," was his only comment.

Helen Hayes, On Reflection

10 Reputed Aphrodisiacs

Oysters

Cayenne Pepper

Power

Cinnamon
(to the ancient Egyptians)

Ginseng

Zinc
(for men)

Figs

Perfume

Garlic

Diamonds
(for women)

SONNET #43

How do I Love thee? Let me count the ways.
I love thee to the depth and breadth and height
My soul can reach, when feeling out of sight
For the ends of Being and ideal Grace.
I love thee to the level of everyday's
Most quiet need, by sun and candle-light.
I love thee freely, as men strive for Right;
I love thee purely, as they turn from Praise.
I love thee with the passion put to use
In my old griefs, and with my childhood's faith.
I love thee with a love I seemed to lose
With my lost saints,—I love thee with the breath,
Smiles, tears, of all my life!—and, if God choose,
I shall but love thee better after death.

Elizabeth Barrett Browning, Sonnets from the Portuguese

Love one another, but make not a bond
      of love
Let it rather be a moving sea between
      the shores of your souls.
Fill each other's cup but drink not from
      one cup.
Give one another of your bread but eat
      not from the same loaf.
Sing and dance together and be joyous,
      but let each one of you be alone
      though they quiver with the same music.

Kahlil Gibran, The Prophet

Come live with me and be my love . . .

HERE WE ARE IN OUR SUMMER YEARS
LIVING ON ICE-CREAM AND CHOCOLATE KISSES.
BUT WOULD THE LEAVES FALL FROM THE TREES
IF I WAS YOUR OLD MAN
AND YOU WAS MY MISSUS?

Billy Bragg, "Greetings to the New Brunette"

THE YOUNGER GENERATION, WHO HAVE A TASTE FOR,
WHO SEE IDEAL BEAUTY IN NAKEDNESS — FROM DANCERS
WITH BARE FEET TO THE SO-CALLED NAKED TRUTH IN
ALL RELATIONSHIPS — OPENLY ENTER INTO THEIR
MARRIAGES AS LOVE AFFAIRS AND CELEBRATE THEIR
WEDDINGS AS FESTIVALS OF LOVE.

Isak Dinesen, On Modern Marriage and Other Observations

MARRIAGE IS THE PERFECTION WHICH LOVE AIMED AT,
IGNORANT OF WHAT IT SOUGHT.

Ralph Waldo Emerson, Journals

WHEN I THINK WHAT LIFE IS, AND HOW SELDOM LOVE
IS ANSWERED BY LOVE — MARRY HIM; IT IS ONE OF THE
MOMENTS FOR WHICH THE WORLD WAS MADE.

E. M. Forster, A Room with a View

Keep your eyes wide open before marriage,
half shut afterward.

Benjamin Franklin, Poor Richard's Almanac

Marriage is popular because it combines
the maximum of temptation with the
maximum of opportunity.

Bernard Shaw, Man and Superman

Marriage is a wonderful invention,
but, then again, so is a bicycle repair kit.

Billy Connolly, in Billy Connolly *quoted by Duncan Campbell*

But there was Mark. With his big brown eyes and his sweetheart roses. Forever and ever, he said. . . . I'll be loving you always. . . . Not for just an hour, not for just a day, not for just a year, but always.

For a long time, I didn't believe him. And then I believed him. I believed in change. I believed in metamorphosis. I believed in redemption. I believed in Mark. My marriage to him was as willful an act as I have ever committed; I married him against all the evidence. I married him believing that marriage doesn't always work, that love dies, that passion fades, and in so doing I became the kind of romantic only a cynic is capable of being.

Nora Ephron, Heartburn

*M*y head, my heart, mine eyes,
my life, nay more,
My joy, my magazine of earthly store . . .

Anne Bradstreet, "A Letter to Her Husband, Absent upon Public Employment"

Love not me for comely grace,
For my pleasing eye or face,
Nor for any outward part:
No, nor for a constant heart!
For these may fail or turn to ill:

So thou and I shall sever.
Keep therefore true a woman's eye,
And love me still, but know not why!
So hast thou the same reason still
to dote upon me ever.

Anonymous

Camerado, I give you my hand!
I give you my love more precious than money,
I give you myself before preaching or law;
Will you give me yourself? Will you come travel with me?
Shall we stick by each other as long as we live?

Walt Whitman, "Song of the Open Road"

Architect Christopher Wren's feathered namesakes are also architects, if not as famous for their designs. The English wren begins building a nest before he has a mate. Not satisfied, he abandons it and starts another one in a different site. Still not satisfied, he abandons the second and begins a third. Learning his trade by trial and error, the wren finally gets the nest right, and it is a thing of beauty. He builds it from spider's webs, grass, lichens, moss and hairs and lines the bottom with feathers. Then he puts a nice roof over the nest and makes a hole just big enough to fit through. Ready to settle down, the male ventures out, advertising his model home until he finds an interested female, whom he takes on an inspection trip to the site. Strutting ahead, he preens himself and coos sweet nothings as the female shyly follows behind, feigning indifference. At the site he shows her excitedly around the manse. If she likes what she sees, the deal is concluded and the two settle in for some serious billing and cooing.

Daniel Kaufman, Astonishing Facts About Animals

10 Animals that Mate for Life

Swans
Wolves
Eagles
Geese
Silverbacked Jackals
Cranes
Doves
Klipspringers
Marmosets
Ravens

The Passionate Shepherd
to His Love

Come live with me and be my love,
And we will all the pleasures prove
That valleys, groves, hills, and fields,
Woods, or steepy mountain yields.

And we will sit upon the rocks,
Seeing the shepherds feed their flocks,
By shallow rivers to whose falls
Melodious birds sing madrigals.

And I will make thee beds of roses
And a thousand fragrant posies,
A cap of flowers, and a kirtle
Embroidered all with leaves of myrtle;

A gown made of the finest wool
Which from our pretty lambs we pull;
Fair lined slippers for the cold,
With buckles of the purest gold;

A belt of straw and ivy buds,
With coral clasps and amber studs:
And if these pleasures may thee move,
Come live with me and be my love.

The shepherds' swains shall dance and sing
For thy delight each May morning:
If these delights thy mind may move,
Come live with me and be my love.

Christopher Marlowe

With this ring . . .

The wedding ring is a traditional symbol of eternal love that dates back many centuries. Formed as a perfect circle, it has no beginning and no end. By some accounts, its historical meaning was somewhat less romantic—signifying the exchange of something of value for possession of the bride. In ancient Egypt, however, as well as more recently among the Anglo-Saxons, the ring seems to have symbolized the husband's trust that his wife would not abscond with his worldly wealth.

The widely practiced custom of wearing the ring on the fourth finger of the left hand arose from an ancient Roman belief that a nerve connected that finger directly to the heart. Later, the connection was said to be a vein, the *vena amoris*.

Even today, much solemn superstition surrounds the ring. Folk wisdom suggests the proper day of the week on which to buy it (never Friday) and how it should be handled (never let anyone try it on; never drop it during the ceremony). Among the mystical powers it supposedly boasts: a sliver of cake passed through it and then placed under the pillow of an unbetrothed young lady will bring dreams of a future husband.

Dearly beloved . . .

VICTORIAN WEDDING
SUPERSTITIONS

Marry when the year is new,
Always loving, kind and true.
When February birds do mate,
You may wed, nor dread your fate.
If you wed when March winds blow,
Joy and sorrow both you'll know.
Marry in April when you can,
Joy for maiden and for man.
Marry in the month of May,
You will surely rue the day.
Marry when June roses blow,
Over land and sea you'll go.
They who in July do wed,
Must labour always for their bread.
Whoever wed in August be,
Many a change are sure to see.
Marry in September's shine,
Your living will be fair and fine.
If in October you do marry,
Love will come, but riches tarry.
If you wed in bleak November,
Only joy will come, remember.
When December's snows fall fast,
Marry and true love will last.

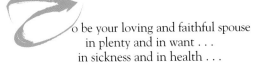

o be your loving and faithful spouse
in plenty and in want . . .
in sickness and in health . . .

Presbyterian

To love and honor you all the days of my life . . .

Roman Catholic

In accordance with the laws of Moses and Israel . . .

Jewish

To laugh with you in joy;
to grieve with you in sorrow;
to grow with you in love;
serving mankind in peace and hope . . .

United Church of Canada

Let us share the joys. We are word and meaning, united.
You are thought and I am sound.

Hindu

To have and to hold, from this day forward, for better, for worse . . .
to love and cherish, till death do us part.

Traditional

Now you will feel no rain, for each of you will be shelter for the other.
Now you will feel no cold, for each of you will be warmth to the other.
Now there is no more loneliness.
Now you are two persons, but there is only one life before you.
Go now to your dwelling to enter into the days of your life together.
And may your days be good, and long upon the earth.

Native American

You say tomato . . .

*Vale más un grito a tiempo que
hablar a cada momento.*

Better one timely squawk than
constant talk.

Jeff M. Sellers, Folk Wisdom of Mexico

Marriage has no enmities which
can survive a happy night.

Chinese Proverb

Marriage is three parts love and seven
parts forgiveness of sins.

Langdon Mitchell, The New York Idea

Love is a battle. Love is war. Love is growing up.

James Baldwin, quoted in the press after his death

If you will ensure a healthy lasting marriage,
always, always value each other. Although you
will disagree, remember to respect each other's
feelings, needs and wants. And above all, never
lose your sense of humor.

Joan Kahn-Schneider, quoted in
For as Long as We Both Shall Live

I pray you if you love me, bear my joy
A little while, or let me weep your tears;

. . .

Let us go forth together to the spring:
Love must be this if it be anything.

Edna St. Vincent Millay, Collected Sonnets, *"Sonnet #28"*

1. Do not expect too much.

2. Continue courting.

3. Moderate your expectations.

4. Be prepared to be disappointed in each other.

5. Bear and forbear.

6. Be willing to make mutual concessions.

7. Try and hide one another's faults.

8. Study to adapt yourselves to one another.

9. Be mutually respectful.

10. Be ready to exercise self-denial.

11. Confide in each other.

12. Row together in the same boat.

13. Resolve to live within your means.

14. Seek the improvement of one another.

15. Have a family altar of your own.

Job Flower, Golden Guide to Matrimony (1882)

And baby makes three . . .

Of all those requirements, which particularly belong to the feminine character, there are none which take a higher rank, in our estimation, than such as enter into a knowledge of household duties; for on these are perpetually dependent the happiness, comfort, and well-being of a family. In this opinion we are borne out by the author of "The Vicar of Wakefield," who says: "The modest virgin, the prudent wife, and the careful matron, are much more serviceable in life than the petticoated philosophers, blustering heroines, or virago queens. She who makes her husband and her children happy, who reclaims the one from vice and trains up the other to virtue, is a much greater character than ladies described in romances, whose whole occupation is to murder mankind with shafts from their quiver, or their eyes."

Mrs. Isabella Beeton, Beeton's Book of Household Management
(originally published in 1859)

Why do fairy tales always end with the prince and princess marrying? Why don't they tell you what happened to the couple in the next fifty years? How did the prince and princess feel when the babies started coming? Did Cinderella ever wake up in the morning to the cry of her baby, feeling as evil and fussy as her stepsisters?

Angela Barron McBride, The Growth and Development of Mothers

My wife and I were suddenly sharing the greatest moment in our lives. This was what we had asked God for; this was what we wanted to see if we could make. And I looked at it lovingly as they started to clean it off, but it wasn't getting any better.

And then I went over to my wife, kissed her gently on the lips, and said, "Darling, I love you very much. You just had a lizard."

Bill Cosby, Fatherhood

I don't know why Alan was so upset when the water broke. I was quite calm. I had things all planned. I marched to the bathroom, piled up the towels, and right away grabbed for the mascara. That was step one in my plan for glamorous motherhood . . .

After I finished with the mascara, I got out my $49.95 genuine Dynel thirty-six-inch fall, wound it into a chignon and started attaching it with forty-seven bobby pins. By this time, Alan had come fully awake and started to panic. I had to shut the bathroom door to keep him from clutching my knees.

"What are you doing in there!" he screamed as I put in bobby pin number forty-eight.

"I'm fixing my hair."

"Oh my God, she's fixing her hair."

"Then I have to find my eye shadow."

"Vei es meir, eye shadow!"

He was pounding on the door with his fists as I lightly dusted it on my lids. By the time I got to the blusher I could hear him sobbing as his fingernails scraped down the outside of the door. Actually, he had bitten off his fingernails, and it was the raw skin rubbing against the pine. I figured it was time to go.

Caryl Rivers, For Better, For Worse

The marriage that I write of in this book has nothing much to do with the lush, romantic visions of my youth. There are squirt guns, not fresh flowers, on my table. There are screams of "I'll tell Mom!", not strains of Bach. There is Diet Rite, not Beaujolais, at dinner. And the answer to "What's new?" is "The toilet seat broke."

Judith Viorst, Yes, Married

Who of us is mature enough for offspring before the offspring themselves arrive? The value of marriage is not that adults produce children, but that children produce adults.

Peter De Vries, The Tunnel of Love

Having kids is a pendulum of exuberance and pixilation, a ticktock of elation and droop. It leaves you breathless and confused. Why, it's almost like being in love.

Hugh O'Neill, Here's Looking at You, Kids

As long as you both shall live . . .

SONNET #10

Oh, think not I am faithful to a vow!
Faithless am I save to love's self alone.
Were you not lovely I would leave you now:
After the feet of beauty fly my own.
Were you not still my hunger's rarest food,
And water ever to my wildest thirst,
I would desert you—think not but I would!—
And seek another as I sought you first.
But you are mobile as the veering air,
And all your charms more changeful than the tide,
Wherefore to be inconstant is no care:
I have but to continue at your side.
So wanton, light and false, my love are you,
I am most faithless when I most am true.

Edna St. Vincent Millay, Collected Sonnets

There is no more lovely, friendly and
charming relationship, communion or company
than a good marriage.

Martin Luther, Table Talk

Between a man and a wife, nothing ought to rule but
love. Authority is for children and servants.

William Penn, Some Fruits of Solitude

To satisfy nature, then, a man need only choose a
woman with whom he can dwell in tranquility under
one roof all his life.

Leon Battista Alberti, I Libri Della Famiglia

Be a lover as they are, that you come to know
your Beloved. Be faithful that you may know
Faith.

Jelaluddin Rumi, "After Being in Love, the Next Responsibility"

TIN WEDDING WHISTLE

Though you know it anyhow
Listen to me, darling, now,

Proving what I need not prove
How I know I love you, love.

Near and far, near and far,
I am happy where you are;

Likewise I have never learnt
How to be it where you aren't.

Far and wide, far and wide,
I can walk with you beside;

Furthermore, I tell you what,
I sit and sulk where you are not.

Visitors remark my frown
When you're upstairs and I am down,

Yes, and I'm afraid I pout
When I'm indoors and you are out;

But how contentedly I view
Any room containing you.

In fact I care not where you be,
Just as long as it's with me.

In all your absences, I glimpse
Fire and flood and trolls and imps.

Is your train a minute slothful?
I goad the stationmaster wrothful.

When with friends to bridge you drive
I never know if you're alive,

And when you linger long in shops
I long to telephone the cops.

Yet how worth the waiting for,
To see you coming through the door.

Somehow I can be complacent
Never but with you adjacent.

Near and far, near and far,
I am happy where you are;

Likewise I have never learnt
How to be it where you aren't.

Then grudge me not my fond endeavor,
To hold you in my sight forever;

Let none, not even you, disparage
Such valid reason for a marriage.

Ogden Nash

I will never forget standing outside my grandmother's candy store in Dayton, Ohio, tears in my eyes, hugging everyone, saying goodbyes. I was a new bride of twenty, headed for some dismal second-floor apartment in Illinois. Always will I remember the last words urgently shouted to me as I was getting into the car. My mother said, "Don't forget to clean the toilets every day"; my grandmother, "Don't put tomato paste in your iron skillet." With that advice I was off to begin my married life . . .

For twenty-one years, I have heard my mother's and grandmother's voices in my head. Never do I put tomato paste in my black skillet. The toilet?—Oh, well . . .

Linda Otto Lipsett, To Love & To Cherish: Brides Remembered

Romance exists in our marriage because we keep it there. Bob knows I care and I know he cares. We tell each other so and we guard our treasure carefully. We work hard to make sure nothing interferes with the lovely feelings we have for each other. We start each day with a hug and a kiss, and if there's something nice to be said, we say it.

Dorothy Greenwald, Learning to Live with the Love of Your Life

The person you've been with so long, whose bed and life you've shared, with whom you've fought and made up, had children, planted gardens, taken walks means more to you than you perhaps know.

William and Jane Appleton, How Not to Split Up

I hadn't fallen in love with Gracie's face, or her legs, or her bust, or her voice or her timing. I fell in love with the whole package. But she did have great timing. And years later, when we were rich, I still loved her. And I still love her today. So whatever my reasons at first, it worked. It worked for a long, long time.

George Burns, Gracie: A Love Story

A good relationship has a pattern like a dance and is built on some of the same rules. The partners do not need to hold on tightly, because they move confidently in the same pattern, intricate but gay and swift and free, like a country dance of Mozart's. To touch heavily would be to arrest the pattern and freeze the movement, to check the endlessly changing beauty of its unfolding. There is no place here for the possessive clutch, the clinging arm, the heavy hand; only the barest touch in passing. Now arm in arm, now face to face, now back to back—it does not matter which. Because they know they are partners moving to the same rhythm, creating a pattern together, and being invisibly nurtured by it.

Anne Morrow Lindbergh, Gift from the Sea

Celebration...

CHAMPAGNE PUNCH

3 RIPE PINEAPPLES

Cover pineapple and juice with:

1 LB. POWDERED SUGAR

Let mixture stand, covered, for 1 hour. Add:

2 CUPS LEMON JUICE

$^1/_2$ CUP CURAÇAO

$^1/_2$ CUP MARASCHINO LIQUEUR

2 CUPS BRANDY

2 CUPS LIGHT RUM

Stir and let stand for 4 hours. Place in a punch bowl with a block of ice.
Stir to blend and chill. Just before serving, add:

4 BOTTLES CHILLED CHAMPAGNE

Irma S. Rombauer and Marion Rombauer Becker, Joy of Cooking

Flowers to Make an Anniversary Bouquet

Globe amaranth: Unfading love
Bluebell: Constancy
Dogwood: Durability
Forget-me-not: True love
Heliotrope: Devotion
Honeysuckle: Devoted affection
Ivy: Fidelity
Sweet pea: Lasting pleasures
China rose: Beauty always new
Red and white rose together: Unity
Red salvia: Forever thine
Stock: Lasting beauty
Veronica: Fidelity
Blue violet: Faithfulness

Kate Greenaway, The Language of Flowers

I'll love you till the seas run dry,

And rocks dissolve by the sun;

I'll love you till the day I die,

And then you know I'm done.

"Who Will Shoe Your Pretty Little Foot"

10 Ways to Celebrate the Day

Spend one night in a fireplace suite at the Ritz-Carlton,
Boston, including champagne, chocolate-dipped strawberries,
morning newspaper and breakfast for two in bed.

Have a custom romance novel created featuring you and your spouse
as the hero and heroine. (Swan Publishing)

Get your spouse's name tattooed over your heart at Erno Tattoo,
San Francisco.

Renew your vows at White Lace & Promises wedding chapel,
Reno, Nevada.

Share a bottle of Dom Perignon champagne.

Take a carriage ride through New York's Central Park.

Present your love with one perfect rose.

Rent *Casablanca*.

Buy a "diamond" ring from a gumball machine
(if you can find a gumball machine).

Have the words, "Happy Anniversary" and your loved one's name
flashed on the scoreboard at Chicago's Wrigley Field during a Cubs
game. (No charge, but no guarantee. Must be mailed seven to ten days
in advance of the date you would like to see it. First come, first served.)

Acknowledgments

"Oh think not I am faithful to a vow!" and two excerpts from "I pray you if you love me, bear my joy" by Edna St. Vincent Millay, from *Collected Poems*, HarperCollins, © 1922, 1923, 1950, 1951 by Edna St. Vincent Millay and Norma Millay Ellis. Reprinted by permission of Elizabeth Barnett, literary executor.

Excerpt from *Folk Wisdom of Mexico* by Jeff M. Sellars, © 1994. Reprinted by permission of Chronicle Books, San Francisco.

Excerpt from *Learning to Live with the Love of Your Life,* © 1970 by Robert and Dorothy Greenwald. Reprinted by permission of Harcourt Brace & Company.

Excerpt from *The Prophet* by Kahlil Gibran, © 1923 by Kahlil Gibran; renewed © 1951 by Administrators CTA of Kahlil Gibran Estate and Mary G. Gibran. Reprinted by permission of Alfred A. Knopf Inc.

Excerpt from *Fatherhood* by Bill Cosby, © 1986 by William H. Cosby, Jr. Used by permission of Bantam Books, a division of Bantam Doubleday Dell Publishing Group, Inc.

Excerpts from *Ruins of the Heart, Selected Lyric Poetry of Jelaluddin Rumi* and *Open Secrets: Versions of Rumi.* Reprinted by permission of Threshold Books, RD 4 Box 600, Putney, VT 05346.

Excerpt from *Cherry Blossoms, Japanese Haiku Series III,* © 1960. Reprinted by permission of The Peter Pauper Press.

Excerpt from *Heartburn* by Nora Ephron, © 1983. Reprinted by permission of Alfred A. Knopf, Inc.

Excerpt from *How Not to Split Up* by Jane and William Appleton. Reprinted by permission of Doubleday, a division of Bantam Doubleday Dell Publishing Group, Inc.

Excerpt from *On Marriage and Other Observations* by Isak Dinesen, © 1977 by The Rungstedlund Foundation; translation © 1986 by The Rungstedlund Foundation. Reprinted by permission of St. Martin's Press, Inc., New York, NY.

Excerpt from *Yes, Married* by Judith Viorst, © 1972. Reprinted by permission of The Saturday Review 1996, SR Publications, Ltd.

Excerpt from *Getting Married & Press Cuttings* by Bernard Shaw, © 1986 by Penguin USA. Reprinted by permission of The Society of Authors on behalf of the Bernard Shaw Estate.

Excerpt from *Claudine Married* by Colette, translation by Antonia White, © 1960; renewed © 1988 by Martin Secker and Warburg, Ltd. Reprinted by permission of Farrar, Straus & Giroux, Inc.

Excerpt from *Joy of Cooking* by Irma Rombauer and Marion Rombauer Becker, © 1931, 1936, 1941, 1943, 1946, 1951, 1952, 1953, 1962, 1963, 1964, 1975 by Bobbs-Merrill. Reprinted by permission of Simon & Schuster.

Excerpt from *Gift from the Sea* by Anne Morrow Lindbergh, © 1955. Reprinted by permission of Pantheon Books, a Division of Random House, Inc.

Excerpt from *I Libri Della Famiglia* by Leon Battista Alberti, translated by Renee N. Watkins. Reprinted by permission of Renee N. Watkins.